A Templar Book

Produced by The Templar Company plc,
Pippbrook Mill, London Road, Dorking, Surrey RH4 1JE, Great Britain.

This edition produced for Parragon Books,
Unit 13-17, Avonbridge Trading Estate, Atlantic Road, Avonmouth, Bristol BS11 9Q

This book contains material first published as
The Wishing Carpet in Enid Blyton's Sunny Stories
and Sunny Stories between 1926 and 1953.

Illustrated by Pamela Venus

Printed and bound in Italy

ISBN 1 85813 372 6

Enid Blyton's

POCKET LIBRARY

THE WISHING CARPET

Illustrated by Pamela Venus

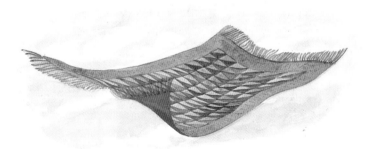

PARRAGON

Once upon a time there were two children who owned a wishing carpet. A little old woman had given it to them in exchange for a basket of flowers. They had met her on Breezy Hill, and she had begged them to give her their basketful.

"Here you are, my dears," she said, when they handed her their flowers. "Here is something in exchange for your flowers. It is a magic carpet. Take great care of it."

They took it home and unrolled it. It was bright blue and yellow, with a magic word written in green round the border. Peter and Sally looked at the carpet in wonder.

"Gosh!" said Peter. "Suppose it really *is* magic!

Sally! Shall we sit on it and wish ourselves somewhere else and see what happens?"

"Yes," said Sally. So they sat themselves down and Peter wished.

"Take us to London," he said. The carpet didn't move. Peter spoke again.

"I said take us to London," he said, more loudly. Still the carpet didn't move. No matter what the two children did or said it just lay still on the floor and behaved like any ordinary carpet.

"It isn't a wishing carpet, after all!" said Sally, disappointed. "That old woman wasn't telling us the truth."

"What a shame!" said Peter.

So they rolled the carpet up and put it right at the back of the toy cupboard. They forgot all about it until about four weeks later when they met a very strange-looking little man in their garden.

"What are you doing here?" demanded Peter.

"Sh!" said the little man. "I'm a gnome. I've come to speak to you about your magic carpet."

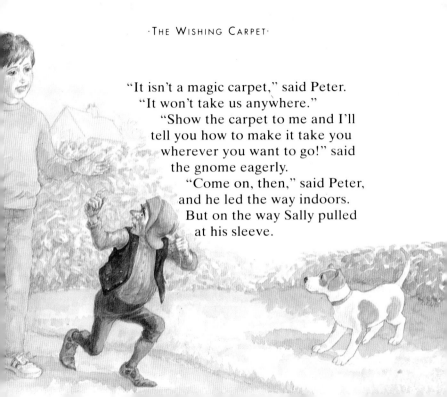

"It isn't a magic carpet," said Peter.
"It won't take us anywhere."
"Show the carpet to me and I'll
tell you how to make it take you
wherever you want to go!" said
the gnome eagerly.
"Come on, then," said Peter,
and he led the way indoors.
But on the way Sally pulled
at his sleeve.

"I don't like that little gnome at all," she said. "I'm sure he is a bad gnome, Peter. I don't think we should show him the carpet. He might want to steal it."

"Don't worry," said Peter. "I shall have a tight hold of it all the time!"

He pulled the carpet out of the toy cupboard, laid it on the floor and then sat on it. The gnome clapped his hands in joy when he saw it and sat down too.

"Come on, Sally," said Peter. "Come and sit down. This is going to be an adventure. Oh look, here's Scamp. He wants to come as well!"

So Sally and Scamp, the puppy, sat down beside the gnome and Peter.

"Did you say the magic word?" asked the gnome.

"Oh, no!" said Peter. "I didn't know I had to."

"Well, no wonder the carpet wouldn't move then!" said the gnome. "Listen!"

The gnome looked closely at the word round the border, and then clapped his hands twice.

"Arra-gitty-borra-ba!" he said. "Take us to Fairyland!"

The carpet started to tremble and then rose in to the air.

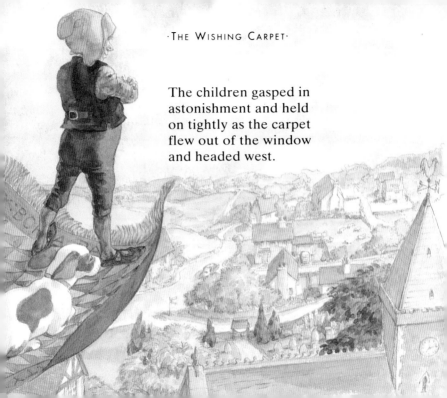

The children gasped in astonishment and held on tightly as the carpet flew out of the window and headed west.

"Oh!" said Peter. "What an adventure! Are we really going to Fairyland?"

"Yes," said the gnome. "Watch out for the towers and pinnacles on its border."

Sure enough, before long the children saw shimmering towers and tall pinnacles on the blue horizon. The carpet flew on, and the world below seemed to flow away from them like a river.

"Fairyland!" cried Sally. "How lovely!"

They soon passed over a high wall, and the carpet flew downwards to a big market square. Then something dreadful happened! The carpet had hardly reached the ground when the gnome pushed Peter and Scamp off. But Sally was still on it with the gnome.

"Ha ha!" cried the gnome. "Now I've got Sally! She will be my servant and I've got the carpet for myself, foolish boy! Arra-gitty-borra-ba! Take me to my castle, carpet!"

Before Peter or Scamp could react, the carpet was flying high above the chimney tops. Peter groaned in despair.

"Oh dear, oh dear, whatever shall I do? I should have listened to Sally. Now that gnome will make her his servant and perhaps I'll never see her again!"

Scamp put his nose into Peter's hand, and to the boy's surprise, the puppy spoke.

"Don't worry, Peter," he said. "We'll get her back again."

"You can speak!" cried Peter in surprise.

"All animals in Fairyland can talk," said Scamp.

Peter looked round the market square. He saw many pixies, elves and brownies. They had seen what happened and came up to speak to Peter.

"Please help me," he said. "A horrid gnome took my sister away on a magic carpet. I don't know where they've gone, but I must get Sally back. She will be so frightened without me."

"That must have been Wily! He lives in a castle far away from here. Nobody dares to go near him because he is so powerful."

"Well, I *must* go and find him," said Peter bravely. "I've got to rescue my sister. Please tell me how to get to Wily's castle."

"The Blue Bird will take you to the land where he lives," said a pixie. "There you will find an old lady in a yellow cottage. She will tell you which way to go next."

Then one of the little folk took a silver whistle from his pocket, and blew seven blasts. In a few moments the sound of flapping wings was heard and a great blue bird soared over the market place. It flew down and the little folk ran to it.

"Blue Bird, we want your help," they cried. "Will you take Peter to the Land of Higgledy? His sister has been carried off by Wily the Gnome and he wants to rescue her."

"Certainly," said the bird. "Jump on."

So Peter and Scamp climbed
up on the Blue Bird's soft,
feathery back. He spread
his wide wings, and flew
off into the air. Peter
held tight, and Scamp
whined, for he was
rather frightened.

After flying for
half an hour, the
Blue Bird turned
his head round
and spoke to
Peter.

"We're nearly there," he said. "Can you see some of the houses?"

Peter looked down. He saw a very curious land. All the trees and houses were higgledy-piggledy. The trees grew twisted, and houses were built in crooked rows. Their windows and chimneys were all lopsided.

The bird flew down to the ground, and Peter and Scamp got off his back.

"Thank you very much, Blue Bird, for your help," said Peter.

"Don't mention it," said the Blue Bird. "Take one of my feathers. It may be useful to you, for whenever you want to know where anything is it will point in the right direction."

"Thank you," said Peter, and he pulled a little blue feather from the bird's neck. He put it into his pocket, and said goodbye. Then he looked for the yellow cottage that he had been told about. It was just a little way off, and it looked as if it might tumble down at any moment.

An old woman stood at the gate.

"Please," said Peter politely to the old woman, "could you tell me the way to the castle of Wily the Gnome?"

"I wouldn't go there," said the old lady. "That gnome is very wicked."

"I know," said Peter. "But he's got my sister, so I *must* find him."

"Dear, dear, is that so?" said the old woman. "Well, you must catch the bus at the end of the lane, and ask for Cuckoo Corner. Get off there, and look for a green flower behind the hedge. Sit on it and wish yourself underground. As soon as you find yourself in the earth, call for Mr. Mole. He will tell you what to do next."

"Thank you," said Peter.

Hearing the rumbling sound of a bus, Peter ran up the lane. At the top he saw a wooden bus pulled by rabbits. He climbed in and sat down with Scamp at his feet. The bus conductor, a duck, asked Peter where he wanted to go.

"Cuckoo Corner," said Peter. "How much is that, please?"

"We don't charge anything on this bus," said the duck, giving Peter a ticket as large as a post card. "I'll tell you when we get there."

Peter didn't need to be told when they had got to Cuckoo Corner because there was a most tremendous noise of cuckoos cuckooing for all they were worth! Peter hopped off the bus, and soon found the green flower.

"I've never seen a green flower before," he said to Scamp. "Come on, boy. Jump on my knee, or you may get left behind!"

He sat down on the flower and wished himself underground. Scamp gave a bark of fright as he felt himself sinking downwards, and Peter lost all his breath. They came to rest in a cave lit by glow-worms. Peter jumped off the flower.

"Mister Mole!" he shouted.
"Mister Mole! Where are you?"
Suddenly a door opened in the
wall of the cave and a mole with
spectacles on his nose appeared.

"Here I am," he said. "What do you want?"

"Please will you help me?" said Peter. "I want to rescue my sister from Wily the Gnome and I don't know what to do next."

"Well, this door leads to the cellars of Wily's castle," said the mole. "Come with me."

Peter followed the mole through the door into a large cellar. The mole led him to some steps.

"If you go up there you'll come to the gnome's kitchen," he said. "Go quietly, someone's there."

Peter listened, and sure enough he heard someone walking about overhead. He felt rather frightened. Suppose it was the gnome?

Peter crept very quietly up the steps – but then, Scamp suddenly whined and darted off.

He disappeared through a door at the top, and
Peter was left alone.

Quietly Peter climbed the rest of the steps.
He thought that he could
hear someone crying.
He popped his head
round the door – and
there was Sally crying
and laughing over
Scamp.

"Sally!" cried
Peter, and he ran
to hug her. How
pleased she was
to see him.

"That horrid gnome brought me to his castle and locked me in this kitchen," said Sally. "He says I'm to scrub the floor and cook his dinner. Oh, Peter, how can we escape from here?"

"I'll find a way!" said Peter, bravely – but just as he said that, his heart sank almost into his boots, for who should come stamping into the kitchen but the wicked gnome himself!

"Ha!" he said in surprise, when he saw Peter. "So you think you'll rescue your sister, do you? Well, you're wrong. There are no doors to this castle, and only one window right at the very top! You can't get out of there! Now I shall have two servants instead of one! You can start work by scrubbing the kitchen floor."

Peter watched in dismay as the gnome locked
the cellar door with a large key. Sally began to cry.

"Don't be frightened," said Peter.

"There must be a way out!" He
searched everywhere but there
wasn't a single door that led outside,
and not a window to be seen.

The gnome came into the
kitchen again. He flew
into a rage.

"Set to work!" he cried. "Fry me some bacon and eggs and make me some tea and toast." He stamped out of the kitchen. All three set to work, and soon the gnome's meal was ready on a tray. Peter carried it up to a tiny room. The gnome told him to put the tray down, and Peter ran back to Sally.

"If we're going to escape, we'd better do it now!" he said. "The gnome is busy eating. If only we knew where the magic carpet was!"

"What about that feather the Blue Bird gave you, Peter?" cried Scamp. "Can't you use that to find the carpet?"

"Of course!" cried Peter. He held the feather up.

"Point to where the magic carpet is!" he commanded.

At once the feather twisted round
and pointed towards the door that led
into the hall.

"Come on," cried Peter. "It will show us the
way!" They all went into the hall. Then the
feather pointed to the stairs. So they crept upstairs.

At last they came to a wide landing. The blue feather pointed to a big chest. Sally opened the chest and inside lay the magic carpet. With a cry of joy she unrolled it. But at that very moment the gnome came rushing up the stairs.

"Ho!" he cried. "So that is what you're doing!"

"Quick!" cried Peter, pulling Sally on to the carpet. The gnome raced up to them, but brave Scamp rushed at the gnome, growling fiercely.

"Keep back or I'll bite you!" snarled Scamp, as the trembling gnome crouched against the wall.

"Scamp, Scamp, come on!" cried Peter. "We must go whilst we can!"

"I can't!" said Scamp. "I'll keep the gnome here while you go. Never mind me."

Peter was sad to leave brave Scamp behind –
but he knew that he must rescue Sally.

"Arra-gitty-borra-ba! Take us home!" he cried.

At once the carpet rose from the ground and
flew upwards. It went up staircase after staircase,
until it came to a big open window right at the
very top. Just then Peter heard Scamp barking.

"Wait, wait!" he said to the carpet. But it
didn't wait. It flew out of the window and began
to sail away to the east. Peter was in despair.

Scamp appeared at the window . He saw the
carpet flying away, and he jumped. It was an
enormous jump, and he nearly missed the carpet!
He wouldn't have landed safely if Peter hadn't
caught his tail and pulled him on.

How happy they were to be going home together! Very soon they were over their own garden, and the carpet flew down to their nursery window. They all jumped off, and danced round in delight.

"Scamp, can you still talk?" asked Sally.

"Wuff, wuff!" barked Scamp.

"Never mind," said Peter. "We understand your barks. What shall we do with the magic carpet?"

"Let's send it away in the air by itself!" said Sally. "*We* shan't want to use it again after all our adventures, I'm sure."

"All right," said Peter. He spoke to the carpet.

"Arra-gitty-borra-ba!" he said. "Rise up and fly round and round the world!"

At once the carpet rose and flew out of the window. It was soon out of sight. And, if you look carefully into the sky on a clear night, sometimes – just sometimes – you can see the wishing carpet still flying round the world.

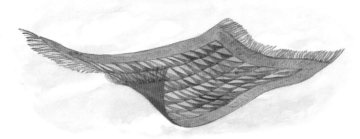